BREAKING THE SHELLS

AF121048

AKOSOTTU

BLUEROSE PUBLISHERS
India | U.K.

Copyright © Akosottu 2024

All rights reserved by author. No part of this publication may be reproduced, stored in a retrieval system or transmitted in any form or by any means, electronic, mechanical, photocopying, recording or otherwise, without the prior permission of the author. Although every precaution has been taken to verify the accuracy of the information contained herein, the publisher assumes no responsibility for any errors or omissions. No liability is assumed for damages that may result from the use of information contained within.

BlueRose Publishers takes no responsibility for any damages, losses, or liabilities that may arise from the use or misuse of the information, products, or services provided in this publication.

For permissions requests or inquiries regarding this publication, please contact:

BLUEROSE PUBLISHERS
www.BlueRoseONE.com
info@bluerosepublishers.com
+91 8882 898 898
+4407342408967

ISBN: 978-93-5704-317-5

Cover Design: Sadhna Kumari
Typesetting: Pooja Sharma

First Edition: May 2024

Dedication

To my beloved wife, Babitha, and our cherished daughter, Aadhea,

This book is dedicated to you both, the heartbeats of my life. Babitha, you are my compass, guiding me through life's storms with your strength, love, and unwavering support. Aadhea, you are our joy, the light that illuminates our days with laughter and wonder. Together, you are my inspiration, my motivation, and the reason behind every word I write.

In the pages that follow, know that every word, every sentiment, is imbued with my love for you both. This journey, marked by its trials and triumphs, is a testament to the beauty and resilience of the life we share. You are my muse, my sanctuary, and the essence of all that I aspire to be.

With all my love,

Akosottu

Acknowledgement

As I sit to pen down these acknowledgements, my heart is full of gratitude and love for those who have been the pillars of strength, not just in the journey of crafting this book, but through the voyage of life itself. This book, a labor of love and perseverance, would not have seen the light of day without the unwavering support of my family and friends, who have been my constant source of inspiration and encouragement.

To my parents, your boundless love and belief in me have been the guiding stars of my life. Your sacrifices, wisdom, and unconditional support have shaped me into the person I am today. Thank you for instilling in me the values of hard work and perseverance, and for showing me the beauty of dreaming big.

To my brother and sister, whose camaraderie and love have been my safe haven in times of turmoil and joy alike. Your unwavering faith in my abilities, even when I doubted myself, has been a source of immense strength. Thank you for being my first critics and my most ardent cheerleaders, teaching me the true meaning of family.

To my wife, the light of my life, thank you for being my partner, my muse, and my biggest supporter. Your patience, understanding, and love have made this journey not just possible, but a journey worth embarking on. You have been the calm in the storm, the joy in my heart, and the reason I strive to be better every day.

To Mithun, Sathya, AJ, Varun, Gautham, Prakriti and Vandana friends who have become family, thank you for the laughter, the late-night discussions, and the endless encouragement. Each one of you has contributed to this book in ways words can hardly express. Your belief in my vision, your constructive criticism, and your unwavering support have been invaluable.

I extend my heartfelt gratitude to Bluerose Publishers for believing in my story and helping me bring my first book to light. Your guidance, professionalism, and dedication to nurturing new voices in the literary world have been instrumental in turning my dream into reality. Thank you for being my partners in this journey, for your patience, and for providing a platform where my words can reach the hearts of readers.

This book is a tribute to all of you, a reflection of the love, support, and inspiration you have generously showered upon me. It is my hope that as you read through these pages, you see the imprint of your influence, for this story is as much yours as it is mine.

Thank you for being my anchor, my compass, and my guiding light. Here's to the journey ahead, to the stories yet to be told, and to the enduring bonds that connect us all.

With deepest gratitude and love,

Akosottu

Preface

In the vibrant tapestry of a bustling city, where every shadow and light tells a story, my journey with Pavitra unfolds—a narrative steeped in love, veiled secrets, and the silent vows that anchor our souls. This isn't merely our story; it's a chronicle of resilience, a testament to the indomitable spirit that thrives within us all, guiding us through life's tempests with love as our unfailing compass.

I, Nakulan, walked a path shrouded in the intrigue of espionage, harboring secrets that bore the weight of altering global tides. Yet, beneath the guise of an adept spy, was a man yearning for the simplicity of domestic bliss and the warmth of love's embrace. My life, a balance between duty and the heart's desires, found its true north in Pavitra—the woman who became not just my partner but my solace, my strength.

Pavitra, the epitome of grace under pressure, held secrets of her own, crafting a delicate balance that kept our worlds intertwined yet apart. Her life, a meticulous arrangement of hidden truths and domestic tranquility, came undone as our intertwined destinies unraveled, revealing the depth of our unseen bonds. Her resilience in the face of adversity, and her unwavering resolve to protect our family, painted her as a beacon of hope and the very embodiment of strength.

Bound by love and thrust into a maelstrom of danger and deceit, our lives took on a new rhythm, punctuated by the laughter and light of Boo, our daughter. Her innocence, a stark contrast to the shadows that chased us, became the anchor that steadied our tempest-tossed souls, reminding us of the purity and hope that love brings.

As the narrative weaves through the quietude of our love and the cacophony of a world on the brink, it delves into the essence of our being—the sacrifices made in love's name, the lengths traversed to shield our cherished ones, and the unwavering faith that guides us through the darkest nights.

This story, set against the backdrop of looming global upheaval, transcends the realms of espionage and domesticity, probing the depths of what it means to choose love, to face the specter of loss, and to fight for a sliver of hope in a future together. It poses a question to the soul: What are we willing to risk, to sacrifice, for the promise of a dawn shared with those we hold dear?

As you journey through our lives, through the trials and triumphs that define us, you embark on an exploration of human connection, the sacrifices entailed in a life led in shadows, and the relentless hope that love ignites, even amidst despair.

As I reflect on the path that has led me here, I can't help but marvel at the intricate dance of fate and choice that has woven the fabric of our lives together. This journey, mine and Pavitra's, intertwined with threads of secrecy and illuminated by the light of our love, has been nothing short of a testament to the enduring power of the human spirit.

Our story is not just a narrative of two individuals caught in the whirlwind of life's unpredictability; it's a deeper exploration of the sacrifices we're willing to make in the name of love and the strength we find in each other when faced with seemingly insurmountable challenges. It's about the moments of vulnerability that reveal our true strength, and the realization that in love, we find our greatest ally against the world's trials.

The journey began in the seemingly mundane corridors of our office, a place where our initial exchanges, simple and unassuming, laid the groundwork for a connection that would defy the ordinary. Pavitra, with her serene grace and piercing intellect, became the mystery I was compelled to unravel, the force that drew me into a world far removed from the espionage that cloaked my existence. Her presence introduced a depth to life I hadn't known, turning every shared moment, every whispered conversation, into a milestone in our evolving bond.

As the reality of my double life came to light, the world we had built together was thrust into chaos, challenging the very foundation of our trust and love. The irony of our parallel secrets, each designed to protect the other yet inadvertently causing pain, was a stark reminder of the complexities of love entwined with duty. The revelation was a crucible, testing our resolve, our love, and our commitment to the future we envisioned.

Facing the adversities of my illness, the relentless battle against cancer, we discovered the profound truth that it is not the suffering that defines us, but our response to it. The grueling months of chemotherapy, the physical and emotional toll it exacted, were dark chapters in our story. Yet, it was within this darkness that we found our most luminous strength—the love and support that bound us, the shared hope for a brighter tomorrow.

Pavitra, in her unwavering determination to protect our family and unearth the truth of my disappearance, embodied the essence of resilience. Her journey from the tranquility of our home to the forefront of a battle she never anticipated is a narrative of courage, a reflection of the depth of her love, and a demonstration of the indomitable will to fight for those we hold dear.

As our home transformed into a fortress, a sanctuary against the encroaching shadows, the solidarity of our family and friends shone as a beacon of hope. Their support, a testament to the impact of our lives entwined with theirs, became our strength, fueling our resolve to face the uncertainties of tomorrow together.

Our story is more than a tale of espionage and domestic trials; it's a celebration of the human spirit's capacity to transcend the confines of circumstance, to find light in the darkest of times, and to forge unbreakable bonds through the power of love. It's an invitation to journey with us, to witness the extraordinary resilience that lies in the heart of every ordinary moment, and to discover the unseen bonds that connect us all.

As you delve deeper into our lives, into the heart of our story, may you find reflections of your strength, hope, and the unyielding power of love that binds us, even in the face of life's greatest storms. Welcome to our continuing saga, a narrative that seeks to unfold the boundless possibilities of love, resilience, and the enduring promise of a shared tomorrow.

Contents

Chapter 1: Fire 1

Chapter 2: Earth 8

Chapter 3: Water 17

Chapter 4: Air 23

Chapter 5: Sky 40

Chapter 1: Fire

---※---

As I walked through the bustling heart of the city, my mind replayed every moment, every glance exchanged with Pavitra. The office, with its relentless rhythm of calls and keyboard clicks, had become a stage for an unexpected play in which I found myself the unwitting protagonist. There was something about Pavitra that stood in stark contrast to the monotony of our office life. Her elegance, embodied in the simplicity of a black churidar, seemed to pull me in, a beacon in the midst of our mechanical existence.

I had always prided myself on being the office charmer, the one who could lighten the mood with a quick joke or a casual smile. Yet, standing before Pavitra, all my confidence seemed to falter. Our first conversations were awkward dances, steps misaligned, but with each faltering move, we were slowly finding our rhythm. It wasn't just her beauty that captivated me; it was the fierce intelligence that shone in her eyes, the quick wit that kept me on my toes.

As the weeks unfolded, my affection for her deepened. I found myself lingering in the office long after my work was done, just to share a few more moments with her. The small gestures—bringing her favorite coffee, sharing a laugh—became the highlights of my day. I even orchestrated a team outing with the secret hope of seeing her light up in a setting away from the fluorescent lights of our office. With every shared smile, every whispered joke, it felt as if we were weaving a connection, delicate yet strong, drawing us ever closer.

Our burgeoning friendship didn't go unnoticed. My colleagues, long accustomed to my laid-back demeanor, began to tease me, their comments a mix of encouragement and curiosity. They saw the change in me, from the office jester to a man singularly focused on one person. Their observations only confirmed what I felt deep within—that what was growing between Pavitra and me was something profound, something that transcended the ordinary.

Walking under the soft glow of the street lamps that evening, I found myself rehearsing the words I longed to say to her. The bustling city around me felt like a distant echo, my heart beating to the rhythm of an unseen drummer. I was about to take a leap, to voice the feelings that had quietly taken root in the depths of my soul. The anticipation of this confession filled me with a heady mix of fear and excitement. I knew that what I felt for Pavitra was more than a fleeting attraction; it was a connection that promised to alter the course of our lives.

In that moment, the city, with its endless energy and noise, seemed to pause, holding its breath for the words I was yet to speak. I was acutely aware of the significance of this confession, not just for Pavitra and me but for the narrative of our lives. The office, a place of routine and predictability, had become the setting for a story rich with emotion and unexpected connections. As I practiced my lines, stepping into the unknown, I realized that our tale was a testament to the heart's incredible ability to find its counterpart, a narrative that defied the ordinary and embraced the extraordinary.

That evening, as the city's heartbeat melded with my own, a torrent of thoughts and emotions coursed through me. Reflecting on the days and weeks that had led to this moment, I could scarcely believe the transformation within me. The office, a place I had navigated with ease and casual charm, had become a labyrinth of emotions, with Pavitra at its center.

Her arrival had sparked something unexpected, a shift in my world. In the beginning, our interactions were like tentative steps into uncharted waters, each of us hesitant, unsure. Yet, there was an undercurrent of something more, a pull that neither of us could ignore. Pavitra, with her serene grace and sharp intellect, had intrigued me in ways I hadn't thought possible. It was as if her presence had unveiled a depth to life that I had been oblivious to.

In my efforts to bridge the gap between us, I found joy in the smallest of gestures—staying back to walk with her, surprising her with her favorite coffee, the shared laughter that seemed to resonate deeper each time. These moments, seemingly inconsequential, had woven a tapestry of connection that enveloped us both. And as the bond deepened, I noticed the subtleties of her expressions, the light in her eyes when she smiled, the thoughtful furrow of her brow. Pavitra had become a mystery I yearned to unravel, a story I wanted to be a part of.

The journey from awkward silences to meaningful conversations had not gone unnoticed. My colleagues, ever observant, had watched the transformation unfold. Their teasing, once a source of amusement, now served as a reflection of the changes within me. I had evolved from the office's perpetual jester to someone deeply moved by the presence of another. Their remarks, though playful, echoed my inner turmoil—was I ready to confront the depth of my feelings?

Now, walking under the canopy of the night sky, the city's vibrant pulse echoing around me, I felt the weight of the words I was about to speak. The rehearsed lines, crafted with care, seemed both inadequate and monumental. This was more than a confession; it was an unveiling of my soul, a step towards a future I hoped to share with Pavitra.

The thought of what lay ahead was daunting. In revealing my feelings, I was exposing myself to the possibility of rejection, of altering our relationship irreversibly. Yet, the possibility of not expressing the truth of my heart was a risk far greater. Pavitra had unknowingly become the axis on which my world turned, her smile the beacon that guided me through the tumult of my emotions.

As I neared our usual meeting spot, the rehearsed words played like a mantra in my mind. The luminous glow of the street lamps cast long shadows, mirroring the flicker of hope and apprehension within me. This moment, suspended in the twilight of possibilities, felt like a threshold to a new beginning.

The city, with its endless stories and whispered secrets, seemed to stand still for us. In the grand tapestry of life's encounters, ours was a thread of vibrant hues, a connection forged in the mundane corridors of an office yet destined to transcend the ordinary bounds of friendship.

Taking a deep breath, I steadied my nerves, the rehearsed lines a steady drumbeat in my heart. Tonight, under the cover of the city's embrace, I would reveal my heart to Pavitra, stepping into the unknown with the hope of a shared future. The path ahead was uncertain, but the journey, with all its twists and turns, was one I longed to embark on with her by my side.

As the city's pulse melded with the rhythm of my own heart, I was vividly reminded of the moments that had led me here, to this decisive evening with Pavitra. Each memory, a stitch in the fabric of our shared narrative, brought me closer to revealing my heart. From the monotonous hum of our office, a space transformed by her presence, to the laughter we shared over simple coffee breaks, every instance was a step away from the ordinary, drawing us into an uncharted territory of connection and affection.

I recalled the day when a sudden rain had caught us unprepared, forcing us to share an umbrella. The closeness, the shared smiles as we navigated through crowded streets, offered a glimpse into a life beyond the confines of our workplace. Then there was the team outing, a day out in the sun where I saw her in a new light, her laughter more infectious, her spirit free and untethered. These moments, though fleeting, had etched a profound impact on me, highlighting the depth of my affection for her.

Even the playful banter with my colleagues, once a source of amusement, had taken on a new meaning. Their teasing, a reflection of the change they observed in me, only solidified my resolve. They too had noticed the shift, the singular focus that Pavitra had inspired in me. It was a testament to the transformation within, a metamorphosis fueled by the genuine connection we shared.

Walking through the city that evening, each step took me through a montage of these memories, a reassurance of the journey Pavitra and I had inadvertently embarked upon. The vibrant energy of the city, with its endless possibilities, mirrored my own turmoil and anticipation. As I rehearsed the confession in my mind, the words seemed to take on a life of their own, driven by the sincerity and depth of my feelings.

Approaching our usual meeting spot, I was acutely aware of the significance of this moment. The city, with its ambient noise and bustling life, faded into a backdrop for the scene that was about to unfold. There she stood, her presence a calming force in the whirlwind of my emotions. The exchange of glances, the shared understanding that passed between us, was a silent prelude to the confession that followed.

With each word spoken from the heart, the walls I had built crumbled, revealing the raw truth of my emotions. Pavitra's reaction, a mixture of surprise and warmth, was a balm to my anxious soul. Her words in response, acknowledging the depth of our bond and her own feelings, were like the missing pieces of a puzzle falling into place. It was a mutual revelation, a moment of vulnerability that bridged our hearts even closer.

That evening, as we walked through the city together, the realization of our newfound connection enveloped us in a bubble of contentment and hope. The real-life moments we had shared, from the spontaneous to the mundane, had woven a tapestry of affection and understanding that now promised to guide us into a future filled with shared dreams and possibilities.

Our story, enriched by the tapestry of real-life moments, stood as a beacon of hope in the unpredictable journey of life. It was a reminder that amidst the ordinary, extraordinary bonds can form, transforming lives in ways unimaginable. As we ventured into this new chapter together, hand in hand, the city around us seemed to echo our optimism, its vibrant energy a reflection of the journey of discovery, love, and companionship that lay ahead.

Chapter 2: Earth

As the calendar pages turned, my fascination with Pavitra deepened into something I could only describe as profound. I found myself on a mission to fill her world with moments of unexpected joy, to show her a tapestry of life she hadn't yet experienced. Our weekdays, often swallowed by the relentless pace of office life, were punctuated with surprise lunches, little islands of tranquility in the sea of chaos. Weekends became our escape; I took her on drives through the countryside, where the lushness of nature unfolded before us, a vivid contrast to the urban sprawl we were accustomed to. Watching her face light up at the sight of the serene landscapes, I felt a connection that was both exhilarating and grounding.

Yet, beneath the surface of these shared moments, I sensed Pavitra's hesitation. The joy in her eyes was occasionally shadowed by a depth of concern I hadn't fully understood until one day, she laid bare her fears. Her words, though spoken softly, landed with the weight of the world on my shoulders. She spoke of her family's expectations, of the importance they placed on stability and a respectable career. Her honesty revealed the crossroads we had arrived at: her heart versus her heritage.

The gravity of her revelation was a jolt to my system. It crystallized the depth of my feelings for her and the lengths I was willing to go to ensure our paths remained entwined. Love, I realized, was more than shared laughter and stolen moments; it was also about sacrifices and bold choices. And so, with a heart both heavy and hopeful, I made the decision that would alter the course of our story. I chose to step into the unknown, to leave behind the familiar contours of our city and my current job for the uncertain promise of a future in the IT industry—a future where I could stand by Pavitra, unburdened by the weight of her family's disapproval.

The transition was anything but easy. The road to reinventing oneself is fraught with hurdles, and many a time, the light at the end of the tunnel seemed more an illusion than a reachable goal. But the image of Pavitra's smile, the sound of her laughter, became the beacon that guided me through. Each challenge I faced, each setback, was countered with the unwavering resolve to build a life worthy of her.

When the call finally came, the one that marked the culmination of countless applications, interviews, and anxious waits, it felt surreal. I had secured a position at a promising startup in a new city, a place pulsating with opportunities and challenges. My heart raced as I shared the news with Pavitra, my voice a cocktail of excitement and nervous anticipation. On the other end of the line, her silence spoke volumes. When she finally spoke, her voice was a cascade of emotions—relief, fear, admiration, and an undercurrent of apprehension about the future we were stepping into.

Pavitra's reaction was a mirror to my own turmoil. Her appreciation for the lengths I had gone to was tinged with the fear of the unknown. We stood at the threshold of a new chapter, our future a blank page waiting to be written. The sacrifices made and the challenges faced were testaments to the strength of our bond, a bond that was ready to weather the storms of change. As I prepared to embark on this new journey, the city that had been the backdrop of our love story receded into the distance, giving way to new horizons that promised a life built on love, sacrifice, and the unyielding hope for a shared tomorrow.

The journey to the new city marked the beginning of a chapter filled with apprehension and hope. As the landscapes outside the window shifted, so did the emotions within me. The decision to leap into the unknown for love was both exhilarating and daunting. The bustling new city, with its towering skyscrapers and endless streams of people, was a far cry from the familiar streets and faces I had left behind. But the promise of a future with Pavitra, of a life where we could be together without the shadow of familial expectations looming over us, made every mile traveled away from home worth it.

Starting anew in the IT industry was like learning to navigate a foreign land. The language of codes and digital interfaces was dense and complex, but driven by the vision of Pavitra's smile, I threw myself into the work with a fervor I hadn't known I possessed. The nights were long, often bleeding into the early hours of the morning, as I wrestled with new concepts and technologies. The initial months were a blur of challenges, each day a test of my resolve. Yet, with each hurdle crossed, I felt a step closer to Pavitra, to building a world where our love was not defined by societal norms but by the strength of our commitment to each other.

The day I received my first paycheck marked a milestone. It was a tangible symbol of the new life I was building, of the sacrifices and hard work starting to bear fruit. I remember holding the envelope, feeling the weight of its significance. It wasn't just money; it was a key to unlocking the future Pavitra and I dreamed of. I called her, excitement bubbling in my voice as I shared the news. Her laughter, bright and clear over the phone, was a balm to the exhaustion and a reminder of why every challenge was worth overcoming.

The months rolled on, and with each passing day, I grew more adept at my job. The unfamiliar city started to feel like home, its rhythm synchronizing with the beat of my own heart. But the true north of my compass remained Pavitra. We talked every day, sharing the mundane details and the significant milestones. Her voice over the phone was my anchor, a constant in the sea of change. We dreamt together, weaving plans for the future, our conversations a tapestry of hope and love.

However, the distance was a constant adversary. The digital connection, though a lifeline, couldn't replicate the warmth of her presence, the light in her eyes. I found myself counting the days until we could be together in the same city, under the same roof. The thought of proposing to her, of finally asking her to start a new chapter with me, became a recurring dream.

And then, the opportunity presented itself. The startup I worked for announced a celebration for a successful project completion. It was the perfect moment to bring our worlds together. With a heart full of hope and a plan in motion, I invited Pavitra to visit. The anticipation of her arrival filled the days with a nervous energy. I wanted everything to be perfect, to show her the life we could have together.

When she arrived, the city seemed to sparkle a little brighter. Seeing her step off the train, her face lighting up at the sight of me, was a moment etched in eternity. The weekend was a whirlwind of shared experiences in the new city that I was beginning to call home. I showed her the quaint cafes, the bustling markets, and the serene parks where I had envisioned us spending lazy afternoons together.

On the last night of her visit, under a canopy of stars, I took her hand in mine. The city around us hummed with life, but at that moment, it felt like we were the only two souls in existence. With a voice steadied by love and a heart beating a symphony of hope, I asked Pavitra to marry me, to join me in this new city, and to be my partner in the adventure of building a life together.

Her yes was a whisper that carried the weight of a thousand promises. It was the beginning of a new journey for us, one that we would embark on together, with the city as our witness and love as our guide. The challenges of the past months faded into the background, overshadowed by the joy of our shared future.

The road ahead would not be without its hurdles, but with Pavitra by my side, I knew there was nothing we couldn't face together. The new city, once a landscape of challenges, had become the backdrop to our love story, a testament to the journey of change, sacrifice, and unwavering hope that had led us to each other.

As we embarked on this new chapter together, the city's sprawling skyline became a symbol of our burgeoning life together, each towering skyscraper a testament to the possibilities that lay ahead. The vibrancy of the city, with its pulsating energy and diverse tapestry of people, mirrored the excitement and complexity of our journey. It was here, in this bustling metropolis, that Pavitra and I would lay down the roots of our future, weaving our dreams into the fabric of its streets and avenues.

The challenges of adapting to a new city were paralleled by the exhilaration of discovering it together. Each weekend became an exploration, a chance to uncover the hidden gems and secret corners that would become the landmarks of our shared story. From cozy coffee shops tucked away in quiet alleys to the panoramic beauty of the city from its highest vantage points, each discovery was a treasure, a memory etched into the canvas of our relationship.

The transition into the IT industry was a formidable journey, laden with its own set of trials and triumphs. The steep learning curve was a relentless teacher, but it was Pavitra's belief in me that became my unwavering source of motivation. Her encouragement, a beacon of light on the days when doubt crept in, propelled me forward. The satisfaction of overcoming each obstacle was not just a personal victory but a milestone for us both, a step closer to the life we envisioned.

When Pavitra joined me in the city, the pieces of our puzzle began to fall into place. Her arrival brought with it a sense of completeness, transforming the apartment we shared into a home teeming with love and laughter. The process of building our life together, of merging our dreams and aspirations, was a journey marked by compromise, understanding, and an ever-deepening love.

Our evenings were spent in shared contentment, whether exploring the culinary delights of the city or simply reveling in the quiet of our home, each moment was a testament to the strength of our bond. The challenges of distance that had once loomed large were now a memory, replaced by the joy of shared daily experiences.

The culmination of our journey came one crisp evening, under a sky ablaze with stars. The city around us, alive with its nocturnal rhythm, set the stage for a moment that would forever define us. Holding Pavitra's hand, feeling the warmth of her touch, I knew that this was where our future lay. With words that came from the deepest part of my heart, I asked her to marry me, to officially embark on this adventure of a lifetime together.

Her acceptance was a moment of pure elation, a promise of endless possibilities. It was a pledge to face the future together, with all its uncertainties and joys. As we stood there, the city sprawling out before us, it felt as if the world was affirming our decision, wrapping us in the promise of tomorrow.

In the days that followed, our life together in the new city blossomed. We found joy in the mundane, comfort in each other's presence, and excitement in the life we were building. The challenges we faced, from navigating our careers to adapting to our new environment, were tackled with a shared determination, each victory sweeter because it was achieved together.

Our love story, set against the backdrop of a city that was once unfamiliar and daunting, had evolved into a narrative of hope, resilience, and unwavering commitment. The city, with all its challenges and opportunities, had become not just a place we lived in but a reflection of our journey together—a journey that started with tentative steps towards understanding and grew into a shared path towards a future filled with endless potential.

As we looked ahead, the city no longer seemed like a maze of challenges but a landscape of possibilities. Our journey, marked by moments of real-life challenges and triumphs, had taught us the power of perseverance, the depth of our love, and the strength of our partnership. Together, we were ready to face whatever the future held, our hearts and hopes intertwined with the city's ever-changing horizon.

Chapter 3: Water

───── ✼ ─────

As the new chapter of my life in the bustling city began to unfold, one of my most significant milestones was introducing Pavitra to my family. My parents, Gopi and Nisha, along with my siblings and their families, were taken by surprise at the news of my deep affection for Pavitra. Known for my calm and convincing nature, I took it upon myself to bridge the gap between my world and hers. I shared with them the journey Pavitra and I had embarked on, the challenges we faced, and the dreams we aspired to achieve together. Their initial shock slowly melted away as they recognized the sincerity in my words and the genuine love I harbored for her.

Conversely, Pavitra grappled with her own set of fears about introducing me to her family. Her background, steeped in the traditions of a Tamil Brahmin family, presented a formidable challenge. The thought of confronting her family's expectations with our love story filled her with trepidation. Yet, inspired by the steps I had taken to integrate our lives and honor her world, she found the courage to bring our relationship into the light with her family.

The first encounter with her cousin brother was a critical moment, charged with the tension of anticipation and the weight of familial expectations. Standing before him,

I felt the gravity of what was at stake. However, armed with nothing but my sincerity and a deep respect for their customs and values, I managed to convey my unwavering commitment to Pavitra. His nod of approval was the key that began to unlock the acceptance of the rest of her family.

In the years that followed, both our families embarked on a slow but enriching journey of understanding and acceptance. Through small family gatherings, shared celebrations, and open dialogues, we wove the fabric of our united families. My career progress and dedication further cemented my resolve to build a stable future for us. Pavitra, with her strength and love, acted as the bridge that connected our differing worlds, making each challenge a stepping stone towards mutual respect and acceptance.

The culmination of our five-year journey was a moment of profound joy and relief. When both families finally came together at my house, agreeing to our union, it was a celebration of patience, love, and perseverance. The discussions that took place were filled with emotion—a blend of laughter, tears, and heartfelt conversations. Setting a date for our engagement felt like the dawn of a new era, a testament to the power of love in overcoming barriers.

Reflecting on the journey, I marveled at how far we had come. From the early days of uncertainty and individual struggles to a moment of communal joy and acceptance, our story was a testament to the strength of our bond. It wasn't just Pavitra and I who had found love; our families had discovered a new kinship, bridging cultures and traditions in the beautiful tapestry of our united lives.

The path to this moment hadn't been easy. It was paved with challenges, misunderstandings, and the daunting task of blending two distinct worlds. Yet, standing at the threshold of our new life together, I felt an overwhelming sense of gratitude for the journey. It had taught us the true meaning of perseverance, the depth of our love, and the invaluable lesson that when hearts are united in love and respect, no obstacle is insurmountable.

As we looked forward to our engagement and the life that lay beyond, I knew that the challenges we had faced together had only fortified our bond. The future was a canvas of endless possibilities, and together, with our families by our side, we were ready to paint it with the colors of our love.

In the wake of our families coming together, the engagement planning became a microcosm of our journey - a blend of traditions, negotiations, and the shared joy of creating something uniquely ours. Both families, once seated on opposite ends of tradition and expectation, now found common ground in the happiness of their children. The discussions around the ceremony were more than just logistics; they were symbolic of the bridges we had built, the barriers we had crossed.

As we delved into the minutiae of our upcoming engagement, Pavitra and I often found ourselves caught between the joy of anticipation and the weight of what we had achieved. Our evenings were spent in quiet reflection, conversations weaving through our hopes for the future and the challenges we had overcome. It was during one such conversation, under the soft glow of the setting sun, that Pavitra shared her dream of incorporating elements from both our cultures into the ceremony. Her vision was a testament to the journey we had embarked on - one of unity, respect, and love transcending boundaries.

Inspired by her words, we set about creating a ceremony that was a true reflection of our journey. From the selection of the venue to the rituals performed, each element was chosen with care, embodying the essence of our united families. The process was not without its moments of friction; differing opinions and traditions occasionally clashed, reminding us of the delicate balance we were navigating. Yet, these moments were met with the same perseverance and understanding that had brought us to this point. Through open dialogue and mutual respect, we found solutions that honored both our heritages.

As the day of our engagement approached, the excitement within both families was palpable. Relatives who had once viewed our union with skepticism now came forward with offers of help and blessings. It was a heartening reminder of the power of love to change hearts and minds. The engagement ceremony itself was a vibrant celebration, a confluence of traditions that danced together in harmony. As Pavitra and I exchanged rings, surrounded by the people we loved, it felt as though we were not just promising ourselves to each other, but also to the journey ahead, with all its complexities and joys.

In the aftermath of the engagement, as we basked in the warmth of our families' acceptance and love, I couldn't help but reflect on the journey that had brought us here. From the uncertain beginnings to the challenges of blending our worlds, every step had been a testament to the strength of our bond. Pavitra, with her grace and courage, had been my anchor, her love the guiding light through the toughest of times. My family, once hesitant, now embraced her as their own, their acceptance a gift that I cherished deeply.

Looking forward, the path to our wedding and the life beyond was filled with promise. We knew that the road ahead would not be without its challenges, but the engagement had proven that together, we could face anything. It was a new beginning, not just for us, but for our families, now united in their support and love for us.

The story of how we arrived at this point was more than a tale of love; it was a narrative of transformation, acceptance, and the uniting of two worlds. It was a reminder that at the heart of every challenge lay the opportunity for growth and deeper connection. As Pavitra and I stepped into the future, hand in hand, we did so with the knowledge that the journey we had embarked on was about more than just overcoming obstacles; it was about building a life together, one filled with love, understanding, and the unending support of our families.

Chapter 4: Air

Our marriage marked the beginning of a new chapter, one filled with dreams and the promise of a shared future. The simplicity of the ceremony at Pavitra's ancestral home, rooted in tradition and the warmth of familial bonds, contrasted sharply with the grand celebration that my family orchestrated. These ceremonies, in their own distinct ways, symbolized the merging of our worlds, a testament to our journey together.

As we settled into our life in the city, the initial glow of marital bliss slowly began to wane, giving way to the demands of everyday life. My career in the IT sector demanded long hours, while Pavitra, with grace and diligence, took on the mantle of managing our home. What we hadn't anticipated was the strain this dynamic would place on our relationship. The balance between professional responsibilities, family expectations, and nurturing our bond became a source of tension, turning minor misunderstandings into points of contention. The love that had once seemed invincible now faced the test of daily grind and routine.

Yet, amidst these growing challenges, we found a beacon of joy. The birth of our daughter, Boo, introduced a new depth to our love. Her arrival was a celebration of life, a moment that momentarily eclipsed all worries. However, this profound happiness also ushered in new responsibilities, further straining our attempts to maintain equilibrium. Pavitra, already stretched thin by the demands of home, sought my support more than ever. The weight of being a provider, a partner, and a parent was a balancing act I struggled to master.

Our journey took a dramatic turn with the news of my cancer diagnosis. The shock and fear that gripped our family were palpable, drawing us into a collective battle against the disease. Pavitra, in the face of this adversity, emerged as the bedrock of our family. Her strength and resilience, as she juggled the responsibilities of home, Boo, and my care, were nothing short of heroic. The roles we had assumed were reversed; her unwavering support became my lifeline, pulling us closer even as the specter of uncertainty loomed over us.

Over the next two years, as I slowly regained my health, we began to see glimpses of hope, a chance to reclaim the life we had envisioned. Yet, just as we started to navigate our way back to normalcy, fate delivered another cruel twist. My disappearance during a trip to Bangalore plunged our family into turmoil. Pavitra, already bearing the weight of recent years, faced this new crisis with a fortitude that was both heartbreaking and awe-inspiring. Her resolve, now tested beyond measure, was focused singularly on uncovering my whereabouts and ensuring the safety of our family.

This chapter of our lives, filled with love, challenges, and unexpected trials, was a testament to our resilience. The dual ceremonies of our marriage, symbolic of our union's beauty and complexity, had set the stage for a journey neither of us could have predicted. Through the highs of new life and the lows of sickness and separation, our love endured, transformed by experience and strengthened by adversity. As Pavitra navigated the uncertainty of my absence, her strength was a beacon that promised to guide our family through the darkest of times, holding onto the hope of reunion and the continuation of our shared story.

During those grueling months of chemotherapy, the shadow of cancer loomed large over our family, altering the very fabric of our daily lives. The treatment, though a beacon of hope in the fight against the disease, brought with it a myriad of side effects that tested both my physical and mental fortitude. The once energetic and lively atmosphere of our home was replaced by a somber quiet, punctuated by the routines dictated by my treatment schedule.

The physical toll was evident. My body, once capable of enduring long hours at work and playful evenings with Boo, now struggled with the most mundane tasks. The chemotherapy, while targeting the cancer cells, did not discriminate, leaving a wake of exhaustion and weakness that clung to my frame. Nausea became a constant companion, making the act of eating more of a chore than a pleasure. My weight dropped, and with it, my strength ebbed away, transforming my reflection in the mirror into a shadow of my former self.

Hair loss, a common side effect, became a stark, visible symbol of my battle with cancer. Watching my hair thin and fall out was not just a loss of vanity but a reminder of the relentless fight my body was enduring. This physical change was a blow to my identity, each strand lost a reminder of the uncertainty of my future.

The emotional and psychological effects were equally daunting. The fear of the unknown, of what each new round of treatment might bring, hung over us like a dark cloud. The hope for recovery was often overshadowed by the dread of potential relapse, making it difficult to plan for the future or enjoy the present. This emotional rollercoaster took its toll on Pavitra as well. Her unwavering support was my anchor, yet I could see the strain in her eyes, the silent worry that she carried like an invisible burden.

Pavitra became the pillar of strength for both Boo and me, her resilience a constant source of inspiration. Yet, the role reversal was not without its challenges. As she took on the responsibility of caring for me, managing the household, and ensuring Boo's life remained as unaffected as possible, the stress and fatigue were evident. The nights were the hardest, when the quiet of the house allowed our fears and frustrations to surface. It was in these moments, in the stillness of the night, that we found solace in each other's presence, a reminder of the love that bound us together, stronger than the disease that sought to tear us apart.

The journey through cancer treatment was a testament to the human spirit's resilience, to the strength of family bonds, and the power of love to provide comfort in the face of immense hardship. It reshaped our understanding of life, highlighting the fragility of health and the precious nature of time spent with loved ones. As we navigated the challenges brought on by the disease and its treatment, we emerged transformed, more aware of the value of each day, each moment shared, and more determined to face whatever the future might hold, together.

In the swirling vortex of events that followed my disappearance, Pavitra found herself at the helm of our little ship, steering through stormy seas with a determination that belied her inner turmoil. The days turned into weeks, each passing moment a test of endurance, a battle against the growing dread that threatened to consume her. Yet, she stood undaunted, a fortress of strength for Boo, who was too young to understand the gravity of her father's absence.

The house, once filled with laughter and the mundane yet comforting routines of family life, now echoed with an undercurrent of tension. Pavitra juggled the roles of both parents, her days a blur of activity aimed at keeping Boo's life as normal as possible, while her nights were spent in solitude, grappling with the uncertainty of our future. Despite the support of our families, who rallied around her, offering solace and assistance, the weight of my absence lay heavily on her shoulders.

Amidst the chaos, Pavitra found solace in the community we had built together. Friends and neighbors, once casual participants in our lives, now stepped forward as pillars of support, their kindness a lifeline in the tumultuous sea of her daily struggles. It was in these moments of shared humanity that Pavitra drew the strength to face each day, fueled by the collective hope for my safe return.

As the search for me intensified, led by authorities and augmented by the tireless efforts of both our families, the mystery of my disappearance unraveled slowly, each clue a beacon of hope in the pervasive darkness. The ordeal became a testament to Pavitra's resilience, her unwavering faith a reminder of the vows we had taken, in sickness and in health, in joy and in sorrow.

Throughout this harrowing journey, the bond between Pavitra and me, though stretched across miles and silences, remained unbroken. The memories of our life together, from the simple, traditional ceremony in her ancestral home to the elaborate celebration with my family, from the challenges of balancing work and family to the joy of welcoming Boo into our lives, and even through the trials of my illness, these memories became the bedrock of her resolve.

The narrative of our love, tested by time, distance, and fate, evolved into a saga of hope, perseverance, and the indomitable strength of the human spirit. Pavitra, in her relentless pursuit of answers, became a beacon of hope not just for our family but for all who knew us, her story a poignant reminder of the power of love to transcend the darkest of times.

As the search continued, the community's support never wavered, their actions a testament to the impact of our lives intertwined with theirs. The ordeal, while a trial by fire, also served as a forge for stronger bonds, deeper connections, and an unshakeable faith in the power of love and family.

In the quiet moments of reflection, Pavitra held onto the belief that our story was far from over, that the love that had brought us together, which had sustained us through every trial and triumph, would eventually lead us back to each other. With each passing day, her resolve only strengthened a testament to the enduring power of hope amidst the uncertainty of life's storms.

The saga of our love, a tapestry woven from threads of joy, sorrow, and unyielding faith, continued to unfold, a narrative rich with the promise of reunion and the enduring light of hope that no darkness could extinguish. Pavitra, with Boo by her side and our families united in their support, faced the future with a heart full of hope, a spirit undiminished, waiting for the day our family would be whole once more.

Our marriage marked the beginning of a new chapter, one filled with dreams and the promise of a shared future. The simplicity of the ceremony at Pavitra's ancestral home, rooted in tradition and the warmth of familial bonds, contrasted sharply with the grand celebration that my family orchestrated. These ceremonies, in their own distinct ways, symbolized the merging of our worlds, a testament to our journey together.

As we settled into our life in the city, the initial glow of marital bliss slowly began to wane, giving way to the demands of everyday life. My career in the IT sector demanded long hours, while Pavitra, with grace and diligence, took on the mantle of managing our home. What we hadn't anticipated was the strain this dynamic would place on our relationship. The balance between professional responsibilities, family expectations, and nurturing our bond became a source of tension, turning minor misunderstandings into points of contention. The love that had once seemed invincible now faced the test of daily grind and routine.

Yet, amidst these growing challenges, we found a beacon of joy. The birth of our daughter, Boo, introduced a new depth to our love. Her arrival was a celebration of life, a moment that momentarily eclipsed all worries. However, this profound happiness also ushered in new responsibilities, further straining our attempts to maintain equilibrium. Pavitra, already stretched thin by the demands of home, sought my support more than ever. The weight of being a provider, a partner, and a parent was a balancing act I struggled to master.

Our journey took a dramatic turn with the news of my cancer diagnosis. The shock and fear that gripped our family were palpable, drawing us into a collective battle against the disease. Pavitra, in the face of this adversity, emerged as the bedrock of our family. Her strength and resilience, as she juggled the responsibilities of home, Boo, and my care, were nothing short of heroic. The roles we had assumed were reversed; her unwavering support became my lifeline, pulling us closer even as the specter of uncertainty loomed over us.

Over the next two years, as I slowly regained my health, we began to see glimpses of hope, a chance to reclaim the life we had envisioned. Yet, just as we started to navigate our way back to normalcy, fate delivered another cruel twist. My disappearance during a trip to Bangalore plunged our family into turmoil. Pavitra, already bearing the weight of recent years, faced this new crisis with a fortitude that was both heartbreaking and awe-inspiring. Her resolve, now tested beyond measure, was focused singularly on uncovering my whereabouts and ensuring the safety of our family.

This chapter of our lives, filled with love, challenges, and unexpected trials, was a testament to our resilience. The dual ceremonies of our marriage, symbolic of our union's beauty and complexity, had set the stage for a journey neither of us could have predicted. Through the highs of new life and the lows of sickness and separation, our love endured, transformed by experience and strengthened by adversity. As Pavitra navigated the uncertainty of my absence, her strength was a beacon that promised to guide our family through the darkest of times, holding onto the hope of reunion and the continuation of our shared story.

During those grueling months of chemotherapy, the shadow of cancer loomed large over our family, altering the very fabric of our daily lives. The treatment, though a beacon of hope in the fight against the disease, brought with it a myriad of side effects that tested both my physical and mental fortitude. The once energetic and lively atmosphere of our home was replaced by a somber quiet, punctuated by the routines dictated by my treatment schedule.

The physical toll was evident. My body, once capable of enduring long hours at work and playful evenings with Boo, now struggled with the most mundane tasks. The chemotherapy, while targeting the cancer cells, did not discriminate, leaving a wake of exhaustion and weakness that clung to my frame. Nausea became a constant companion, making the act of eating more of a chore than a pleasure. My weight dropped, and with it, my strength ebbed away, transforming my reflection in the mirror into a shadow of my former self.

Hair loss, a common side effect, became a stark, visible symbol of my battle with cancer. Watching my hair thin and fall out was not just a loss of vanity but a reminder of the relentless fight my body was enduring. This physical change was a blow to my identity, each strand lost a reminder of the uncertainty of my future.

The emotional and psychological effects were equally daunting. The fear of the unknown, of what each new round of treatment might bring, hung over us like a dark cloud. The hope for recovery was often overshadowed by the dread of potential relapse, making it difficult to plan for the future or enjoy the present. This emotional rollercoaster took its toll on Pavitra as well. Her unwavering support was my anchor, yet I could see the strain in her eyes, the silent worry that she carried like an invisible burden.

Pavitra became the pillar of strength for both Boo and me, her resilience a constant source of inspiration. Yet, the role reversal was not without its challenges. As she took on the responsibility of caring for me, managing the household, and ensuring Boo's life remained as unaffected as possible, the stress and fatigue were evident. The nights were the hardest, when the quiet of the house allowed our fears and frustrations to surface. It was in these moments, in the stillness of the night, that we found solace in each other's presence, a reminder of the love that bound us together, stronger than the disease that sought to tear us apart.

The journey through cancer treatment was a testament to the human spirit's resilience, to the strength of family bonds, and the power of love to provide comfort in the face of immense hardship. It reshaped our understanding of life, highlighting the fragility of health and the precious nature of time spent with loved ones. As we navigated the challenges brought on by the disease and its treatment, we emerged transformed, more aware of the value of each day, each moment shared, and more determined to face whatever the future might hold, together.

In the swirling vortex of events that followed my disappearance, Pavitra found herself at the helm of our little ship, steering through stormy seas with a determination that belied her inner turmoil. The days turned into weeks, each passing moment a test of endurance, a battle against the growing dread that threatened to consume her. Yet, she stood undaunted, a fortress of strength for Boo, who was too young to understand the gravity of her father's absence.

The house, once filled with laughter and the mundane yet comforting routines of family life, now echoed with an undercurrent of tension. Pavitra juggled the roles of both parents, her days a blur of activity aimed at keeping Boo's life as normal as possible, while her nights were spent in solitude, grappling with the uncertainty of our future. Despite the support of our families, who rallied around her, offering solace and assistance, the weight of my absence lay heavily on her shoulders.

Amidst the chaos, Pavitra found solace in the community we had built together. Friends and neighbors, once casual participants in our lives, now stepped forward as pillars of support, their kindness a lifeline in the tumultuous sea of her daily struggles. It was in these moments of shared humanity that Pavitra drew the strength to face each day, fueled by the collective hope for my safe return.

As the search for me intensified, led by authorities and augmented by the tireless efforts of both our families, the mystery of my disappearance unraveled slowly, each clue a beacon of hope in the pervasive darkness. The ordeal became a testament to Pavitra's resilience, her unwavering faith a reminder of the vows we had taken, in sickness and in health, in joy and in sorrow.

Throughout this harrowing journey, the bond between Pavitra and me, though stretched across miles and silences, remained unbroken. The memories of our life together, from the simple, traditional ceremony in her ancestral home to the elaborate celebration with my family, from the challenges of balancing work and family to the joy of welcoming Boo into our lives, and even through the trials of my illness, these memories became the bedrock of her resolve.

The narrative of our love, tested by time, distance, and fate, evolved into a saga of hope, perseverance, and the indomitable strength of the human spirit. Pavitra, in her relentless pursuit of answers, became a beacon of hope not just for our family but for all who knew us, her story a poignant reminder of the power of love to transcend the darkest of times.

As the search continued, the community's support never wavered, their actions a testament to the impact of our lives intertwined with theirs. The ordeal, while a trial by fire, also served as a forge for stronger bonds, deeper connections, and an unshakeable faith in the power of love and family.

In the quiet moments of reflection, Pavitra held onto the belief that our story was far from over, that the love that had brought us together, which had sustained us through every trial and triumph, would eventually lead us back to each other. With each passing day, her resolve only strengthened a testament to the enduring power of hope amidst the uncertainty of life's storms.

The saga of our love, a tapestry woven from threads of joy, sorrow, and unyielding faith, continued to unfold, a narrative rich with the promise of reunion and the enduring light of hope that no darkness could extinguish. Pavitra, with Boo by her side and our families united in their support, faced the future with a heart full of hope, a spirit undiminished, waiting for the day our family would be whole once more.

In the labyrinth of challenges that cancer treatment and the subsequent turmoil of my disappearance presented, real-life scenarios underscored the philosophies we lived by. Each instance was a microcosm of our larger battle, a testament to the resilience of the human spirit and the strength of our bond.

Adapting to New Roles and Responsibilities

Pavitra's transition from partner to primary caregiver was a profound shift in our dynamic. Real-life moments, such as her learning to administer my medication or sitting up through the night to soothe my pain, were manifestations of her unwavering dedication. These acts of care, though born out of necessity, became rituals that reinforced our connection, transforming our understanding of love and partnership. The philosophy of selflessness and service to others was lived in these daily acts, teaching us that true strength is found in the willingness to bear each other's burdens.

Finding Solace in Small Joys

Our journey through the shadow of cancer was punctuated by moments of simple joy that became our refuge. A shared laugh over a silly joke despite the cloud of chemotherapy-induced nausea, or Boo's innocent antics that brought a sparkle to Pavitra's eyes, were reminders of the beauty that persists in life's darkest corners. These instances were not just breaks from the relentless march of treatment but real-life affirmations of Nietzsche's philosophy that "He who has a why to live can bear almost any how." They reminded us to seek and cherish the essence of life amidst turmoil.

Communication as a Pillar of Strength

The strain of my illness and the uncertainty it brought could easily have driven a wedge between us. Yet, it was through open, heartfelt communication that we navigated these trials. Discussions that stretched into the night, where fears and hopes were shared with equal vulnerability, became our fortress against the chaos outside. This practice of sharing, not just the burdens but also the moments of hope, was rooted in the philosophy that love, in its truest form, is an act of sharing one's entire self.

Cultivating Resilience Through Community Support

The real-life scenario of our families and friends rallying around us, offering not just emotional but practical support, was a testament to the strength of community. From neighbors who brought meals to family members who stepped in to care for Boo, each act of kindness was a thread strengthening the fabric of our resilience. This collective support system was a practical demonstration of the African philosophy of Ubuntu, which emphasizes that "I am because we are." It reinforced the idea that no one navigates life's trials in isolation, and that strength is multiplied when shared.

Embracing Uncertainty with Hope

The search for me, following my disappearance, was fraught with moments of despair and hope. Each clue unearthed, each dead end encountered, was a rollercoaster of emotions for Pavitra. Yet, it was her refusal to succumb to despair, her determination to hold onto hope, that illuminated our path. This real-life saga of searching, of fighting against the odds, was a manifestation of the philosophy that hope is the heartbeat of the human spirit, a force that propels us forward even when the odds seem insurmountable.

Through these real-life scenarios, our journey encapsulated the essence of living philosophies of resilience, hope, and love. They taught us that life's beauty is not diminished by its trials but is made more profound by them. Each challenge, each moment of shared joy or pain, wove the tapestry of our story, a narrative rich with the lessons of love, the strength of the human spirit, and the unyielding belief in the possibility of a brighter tomorrow.

Chapter 5: Sky

The secrets behind the events that unfolded in our once tranquil home reveal layers of deception, covert operations, and the unseen battles waged in the shadows of international espionage. At the heart of this maelic was my true identity as a top-tier spy, a reality unbeknownst to my family, and most poignantly, to Pavitra, who had her covert life concealed beneath the facade of our domestic existence.

The revelation of my identity was not a mere unveiling of secrets but a catalyst for a series of events that intertwined our lives with global machinations far beyond our quiet life. The irony of our dual lives, both shrouded in secrecy for the sake of national security, underscored a profound truth about the nature of espionage – it demands a sacrifice not just from the agents involved but from their loved ones, ensnaring them in a web of perpetual danger and uncertainty.

Pavitra's shock at discovering my double life, juxtaposed with her secret alignment with a smaller, albeit significant, spy agency, unveiled the intricate dance of shadows we had both been part of, unbeknownst to each other. This mirroring of lives led to an unforeseen chasm of deception between us, challenging the very foundation of trust and intimacy we had built.

My disappearance, following what was to be my final mission, was not an act of random fate but a calculated move by adversaries who had been shadowing my activities for months. The mission, cloaked in secrecy, was aimed at averting a looming crisis that threatened to tip the scales of international peace. The whispers of war and political upheaval that infiltrated our home in the aftermath were echoes of a larger, unseen battle being fought in the corridors of power across the globe.

The message that arrived, shrouded in mystery and offering a glimmer of hope, was part of a contingency plan I had set in motion, a breadcrumb trail designed to offer Pavitra a way to trace my steps in the event of my capture or disappearance. This plan, devised amidst the clandestine world we operated within, was a testament to the depth of my love and my determination to ensure her safety and that of our daughter, Boo, even in my absence.

Pavitra's response to the crisis, her transformation from a partner shielded from the harsh realities of my work to the linchpin of our home's defense, showcased the resilience and resourcefulness that defined her. Her ability to marshal our allies, navigate the treacherous terrain of espionage politics, and maintain a semblance of normalcy for Boo was a remarkable feat, fueled by her love and the indomitable spirit that had first drawn me to her.

The solidarity that emerged among our family and friends, transforming our home into a bastion of resistance, was a beacon of humanity amidst the chaos. It underscored a powerful truth – that the bonds of love and family can withstand the greatest of trials, turning even the most unassuming individuals into heroes in their right.

The saga of our ordeal, with its intricate web of secrets, personal sacrifices, and the battle for a future together, was a poignant reminder of the cost of secrecy and the price paid by those who live in the shadows for the sake of national security. Our journey through this storm of deception and conflict was not just a mission to reclaim our life but a fight to preserve the essence of our family, bound by love, resilience, and an unwavering hope for reunion and redemption against the backdrop of a world teetering on the brink of upheaval.

The tranquility that once defined our family's life, nestled within the embrace of the serene forest, was violently upended in the early hours of one fateful morning. The arrival of armed strangers, their intentions unknown but their demeanor menacing, shattered the peace of our home. The air, once filled with the sounds of nature's harmony, now buzzed with the tension of impending conflict. This intrusion marked the beginning of a revelation that would unravel the fabric of our existence.

The revelation of my true identity as one of the world's top spies struck the family like a thunderbolt, particularly Pavitra. The woman I loved, the mother of my child, found herself grappling with a reality far removed from the life we had built together. Her world, carefully compartmentalized to separate her clandestine activities from our domestic bliss, collapsed as the truth of my double life emerged. The irony was not lost on us; we had both lived lives enshrouded in secrets, yet the discovery of each other's true selves unveiled a chasm of deception and mistrust we had inadvertently fostered.

As the news of my disappearance spread, whispers of my last mission and the ominous shadows it cast on international relations permeated the walls of our once safe haven. The home that had witnessed our joys, challenges, and moments of love transformed overnight into a fortified bunker, a bastion against the unseen enemies that now threatened our very existence.

Pavitra, reeling from the shock of my double life, found herself thrust into a role she had never anticipated. Her training, though aimed at a different life, became her armor as she coordinated our home's defense, ensuring the safety of Boo and the myriad of family and friends who sought refuge with us. Amidst the chaos, her resolve became the anchor for those around her, her actions a testament to the strength and resilience that had drawn me to her.

The tension within the house was palpable, as strategy meetings replaced our usual family dinners, and hushed conversations echoed through the corridors, each one a speculation on my fate and the broader implications of my last mission. The gravity of the situation weighed heavily on Pavitra, yet she bore it with a grace and determination that inspired hope in those around her.

The arrival of a cryptic message, purportedly from me, ignited a flicker of hope amidst the despair. This message, vague yet unmistakably tied to the intricate web of espionage that had ensnared our lives, offered a glimmer of possibility that I was still alive, still fighting to return to them. Pavitra, her spirit bolstered by this slender thread of hope, rallied our family and allies. She vowed to leverage every resource, every ounce of her training, to peel back the layers of mystery surrounding my disappearance.

This chapter of our lives, fraught with danger, deceit, and the ever-looming shadow of a global conflict, became a crucible for our family. Pavitra, emerging as the linchpin of our resistance against the forces that sought to divide us, embarked on a mission not just to uncover the truth of my whereabouts but to preserve the sanctity of our family. Her resolve, in the face of overwhelming odds, was a beacon of hope, guiding us through the darkest of times toward the possibility of reunion and redemption.

As our home stood fortified against the encroaching darkness, the bonds of our family, tested by secrets and lies, began the slow process of healing, fortified by the shared resolve to face whatever challenges lay ahead, together. The ordeal transformed our home from a place of peace to a fortress of resilience, a testament to the enduring power of love and family unity in the face of adversity.

In the days following the cryptic message's arrival, our home, now a stronghold against threats both seen and unseen, buzzed with a heightened sense of urgency and purpose. Pavitra, who had once navigated the tranquil waters of domestic life, now steered our family through a storm of geopolitical intrigue and personal peril with unmatched resolve. Her transformation from the woman I knew into the linchpin of our survival was both awe-inspiring and heart-wrenching, a testament to the depth of her love and the strength of her character.

The message, though brief and enigmatic, had rekindled a flame of hope within Pavitra that burned brightly against the encroaching shadows of despair. It became the catalyst for her renewed determination, driving her to sift through the complexities of my last known mission, piecing together the scattered clues in a desperate bid to find a trace of my whereabouts. Her days were consumed by strategy sessions with the security team, poring over maps and intelligence reports, while her nights were spent in quiet contemplation, strategizing her next move in the silent companionship of our daughter, Boo.

Boo, young and bewildered by the sudden upheaval in her world, found solace in her mother's unwavering presence. Pavitra, despite the weight of the world on her shoulders, provided a semblance of normalcy for Boo, her love a protective barrier against the chaos that surrounded us. Their moments together, brief and bittersweet, were punctuated by Pavitra's attempts to shield Boo from the harsh realities that lay just beyond our fortified doors.

As the siege on our lives tightened, the solidarity among our family and friends, those who had become our unwitting allies in this unforeseen war, grew stronger. The house, a bastion of resistance, echoed with the footsteps of those who came to offer their support, their presence a reminder of the life we once shared and the collective hope for a future reunion. Each person, from close relatives to distant acquaintances, brought with them a piece of the world outside, weaving a tapestry of resilience and unity that bolstered our spirits.

The rumors of my fate and the potential for global conflict that my disappearance had sparked continued to circulate, fueling a firestorm of speculation and fear. Yet, within the walls of our home, amidst the strategizing and planning, there existed a singular focus—to bring me back. Pavitra, with a steely determination, rallied our allies, her leadership transcending the personal grief and betrayal she felt, transforming it into a force of collective action.

Amidst this, the lines between friend and foe became blurred, as Pavitra navigated the murky waters of espionage and diplomacy, her actions driven by a mix of professional training and the raw determination of a spouse fighting for her partner's return. The complexity of our situation, intertwined with international stakes and shadowy adversaries, made each day a gamble, each decision fraught with risk.

Yet, through it all, the beacon of hope that the cryptic message had ignited continued to burn brightly. Pavitra's resolve, fortified by the love and unity of our family and friends, became the guiding light in our quest to unravel the mystery of my disappearance. It was a battle waged not just on the physical front but in the hearts and minds of those who dared to hope, to fight against the odds for the sake of family, love, and the chance to reclaim the life that was so abruptly torn from us.

As Pavitra led this charge, her actions inspired not just those within our immediate circle but extended beyond, touching the lives of others caught in the web of this global intrigue. Her journey, marked by courage, love, and an unwavering determination to face whatever challenges lay ahead, stood as a testament to the power of human resilience and the indomitable spirit of a family united in the face of adversity.

www.ingramcontent.com/pod-product-compliance
Lightning Source LLC
LaVergne TN
LVHW061622070526
838199LV00078B/7380